TRUELOVE

For Captain Nemo

A Red Fox Book

Published by Random House Children's Books
20 Vauxhall Bridge Road, London SW1V 2SA

A division of The Random House Group Ltd
London Melbourne Sydney Auckland
Johannesburg and agencies throughout the world

3 5 7 9 10 8 6 4

First published in Great Britain by Jonathan Cape 2001
This Red Fox edition 2002

Printed in Singapore by Tien Wah Press (PTE) Ltd

THE RANDOM HOUSE GROUP Limited Reg. No. 954009

www.randomhouse.co.uk

ISBN 0 09 943305 2

TRUELOVE

Babette Cole

RED FOX

Now they've got that new baby,
they don't want me any more.

Love feels like a warm puppy.

OW!

Love means sharing.

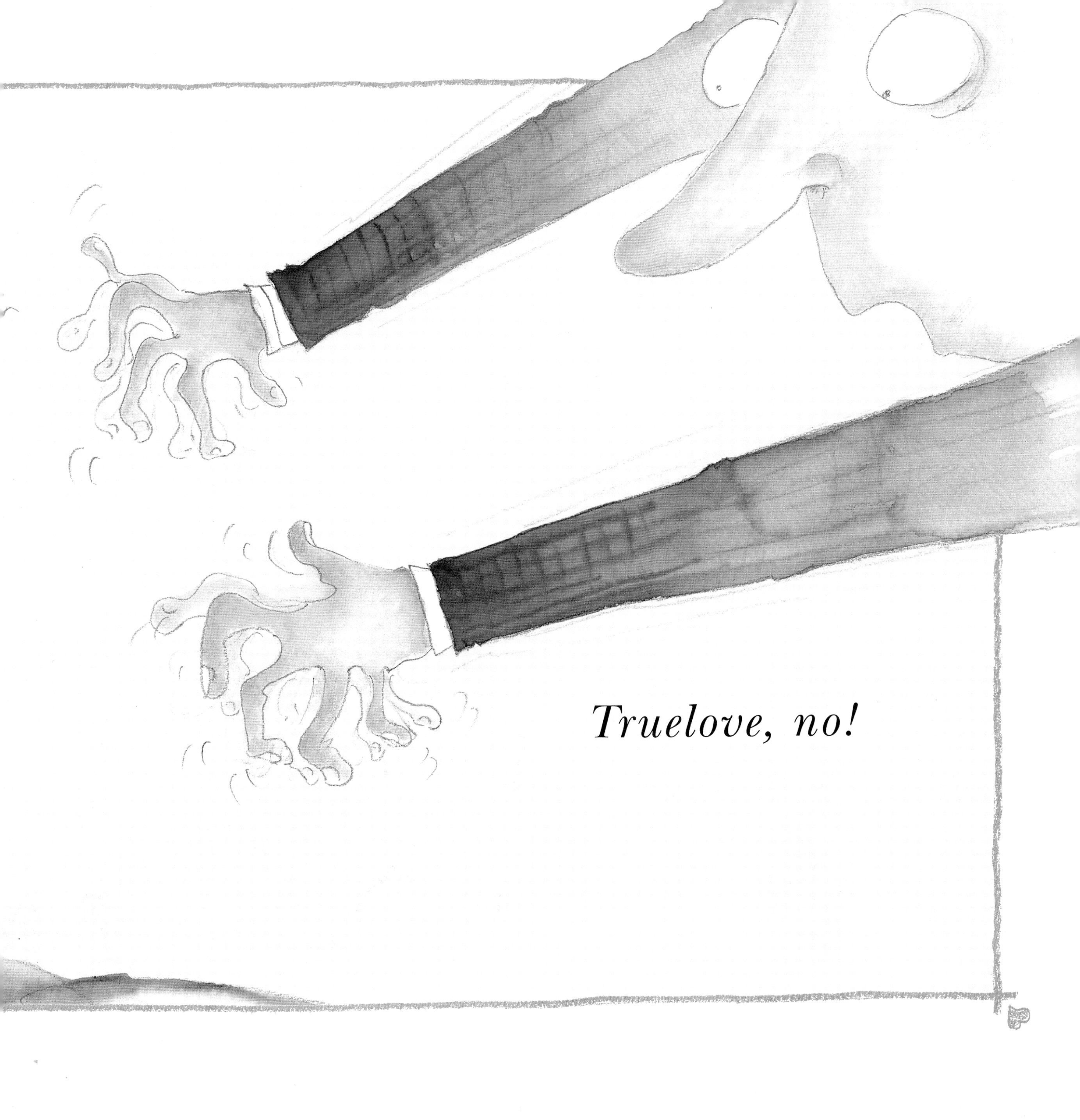

Truelove, no!

Love cures all hurt.

Oh, well.

Love gives you strength.

Truelove!
Put that down!

It makes you notice those you love.

Crash!

Love makes your heart sing.

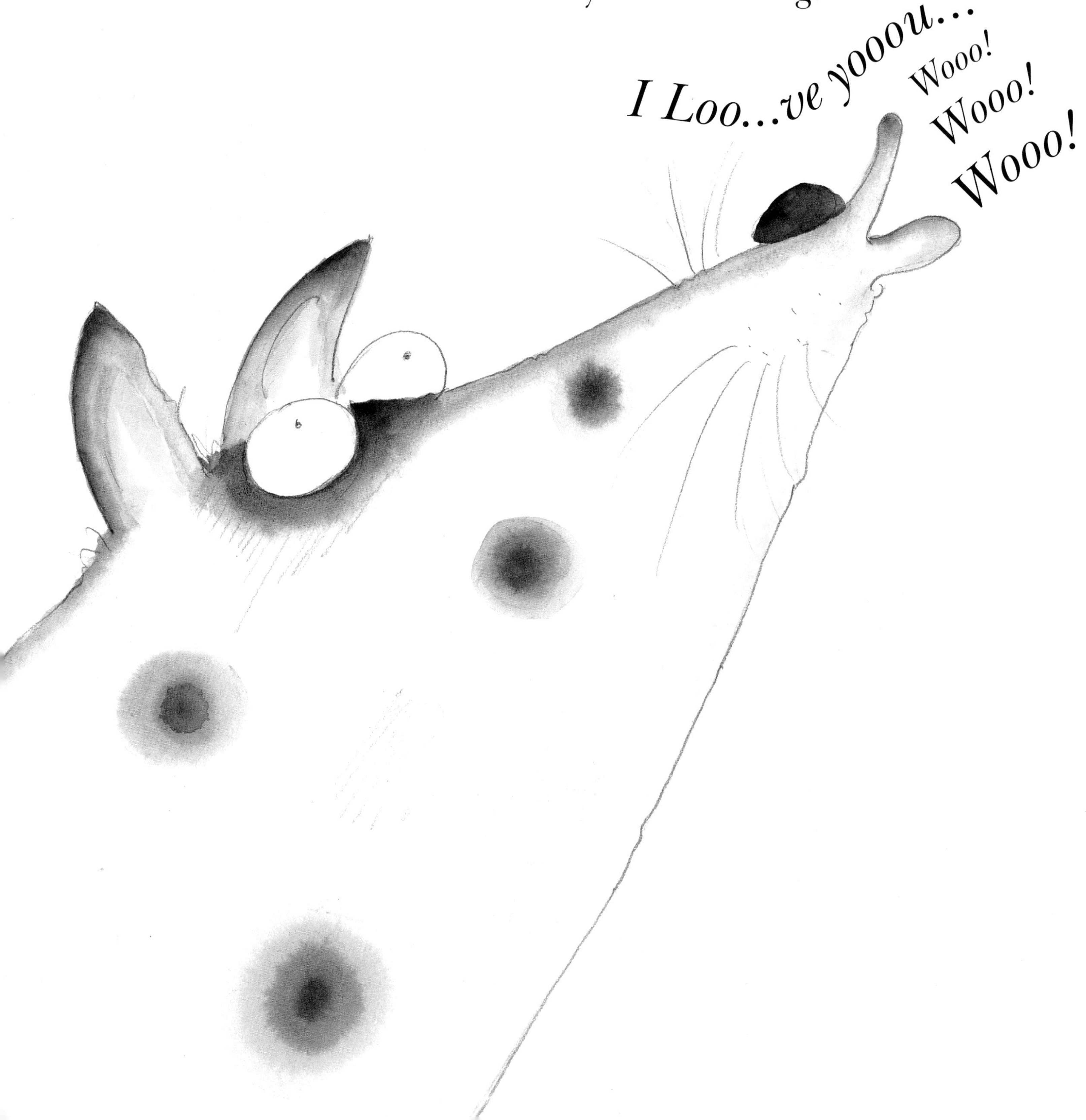

I Loo…ve yooou…

Wooo!

Wooo!

Wooo!

That's it, Truelove. Out!

Love means there's always somewhere
to shelter from the storm.

And like sunshine after rain,
it can lead to a new beginning.

Love means caring for others...

...and being everyone's best friend.

Love makes you do silly things sometimes.

Hey, can anyone drive?

Love sometimes means losing control.

You can never escape from love.

You miss love when it's not there.

Where's Truelove?

Hello, police?

Love is being found when you are lost.

Love means thinking of others.

Of course they can come too.

Love means forgiveness.

We're so sorry, Truelove.
That's OK.

Now I know what love really means.

Other books by the same author in Red Fox

DR DOG

DROP DEAD

THE SMELLY BOOK

THE SILLY BOOK

TWO OF EVERYTHING

MUMMY LAID AN EGG

HAIR IN FUNNY PLACES